Kimberly the Koala Fairy

Special thanks to Narinder Dhami

ISBN 978-0-545-70854-8

Previously published as *Baby Animal Rescue Fairies #5: Kimberley the Koala Fairy* by Orchard U.K. in 2014.

12 11 10 9 8 7 6 5 4 3 2 1 15 16 17 18 19/0

Printed in the U.S.A. 40

First Scholastic printing, January 2015

Kimberly the Koala Fairy

by Daisy Meadows

SCHOLASTIC INC.

The Fairyland Palace
Meadow
Stream
Beehive
Arctic Tundra
Eucalyptus Forest
Tropical Waterfall

Jack Frost's
Ice Castle
To Jack Frost's Zoo
Desert Oasis

Wild Woods
Nature
Reserve
Watering Hole
Pagoda

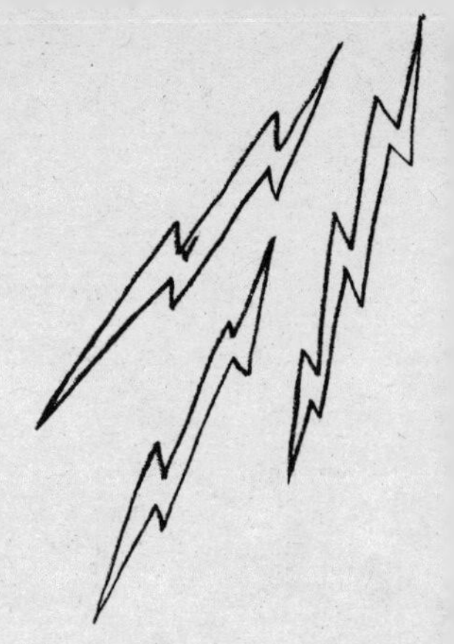

I love animals—yes, I do,
I want my very own private zoo!
I'll capture all the animals one by one,
With fairy magic to help me get it done!

A koala, a tiger, an Arctic fox,
I'll keep them in cages with giant locks.
Every kind of animal will be there,
A panda, a meerkat, a honey bear.
The animals will be my property,
I'll be master of my own menagerie!

Contents

Magic in the Tree

"So, here we are again at Wild Woods. Maybe we'll get another badge today," Kirsty Tate said hopefully, smiling at her best friend, Rachel Walker.

The girls were outside the wildlife center with the other junior rangers. They were all waiting for Becky, the head of the Wild Woods Nature Reserve. Rachel and Kirsty had volunteered to spend a week of summer vacation working at the reserve, which was near Kirsty's home. Every day, Becky gave the junior rangers a job to do. If they successfully completed the tasks, they each received a badge.

"It would be *amazing* to get another one!" Rachel exclaimed, patting her backpack proudly. The girls' hard work had already earned them four badges, and they'd pinned them to the pockets of their backpacks. "It's great to know that we're helping wildlife, and it's really fun, too."

"And helping out at Wild Woods isn't

our *only* job this week," Kirsty reminded Rachel. "We're helping the Baby Animal Rescue Fairies, too!"

When the girls had arrived at Wild Woods at the beginning of the week, they'd been thrilled to discover that their old friend Bertram was there. Bertram was a frog footman from Fairyland and was visiting his relatives. Bertram ended up inviting the girls to visit the Fairyland Nature Reserve with him. The girls had had a wonderful time seeing the animals and meeting the seven Baby Animal Rescue Fairies, who had the job of protecting wildlife everywhere in the human and fairy worlds. The fairies' special magic objects were their tiny animal-shaped key chains. They wore them all the time.

But Jack Frost and his goblins showed up, too. Jack Frost declared that he liked the animals so much, he wanted one of each kind for his own private zoo! When Rachel and Kirsty protested that he couldn't just claim the animals as his property, Jack Frost ignored them. He'd used a lightning bolt of freezing magic to steal the Baby Animal Rescue Fairies' key chains, whisking them away from the fairies and handing them over to his goblins. Jack Frost had then ordered the goblins to go straight to the human world and bring him back some animals for his zoo.

Rachel and Kirsty were horrified! They had quickly offered to help the Baby Animal Rescue Fairies protect wildlife from Jack Frost's selfish plan. The fairies had then combined their magic, waving their wands together to give the girls the power to talk to animals.

"I wonder if we'll help rescue another baby animal today," Rachel murmured. "The four we've met so far have all been so cute!"

Becky came out of the wildlife center, holding a clipboard in one hand and a bag of equipment in the other. "Morning, everyone," she called cheerfully. "I have lots of jobs for you today."

She consulted her clipboard, then smiled at Rachel and Kirsty. "OK, girls, you're first. Follow me!"

Kirsty and Rachel grabbed their backpacks and hurried after Becky into the woodland.

"This is one of our nature trails," Becky explained as they turned down a muddy path that led through the trees. The path was strewn with leaves and twigs. Rachel noticed that the trail was marked by wooden posts with faded yellow arrows on them pointing the way.

"As you can see, it's kind of a mess!" Becky continued. "Today I'd like you to clean up the path for our visitors and repaint the arrows on the trail posts. I'm afraid it's a big job. There are a lot of them."

"We'll do our very best," Kirsty promised. Becky handed her a rake, then she gave Rachel a brush and a pot of bright yellow paint.

"See you later, girls," Becky called and left with a wave.

Eagerly, the two friends set to work. Kirsty raked the leaves into piles at the side of the path, while Rachel began repainting the arrows on the first few trail posts. Then, when they'd finished, the girls moved along to the next section of the trail, and the next.

Rachel was carefully painting yet another arrow, trying to stop the paint from dripping down the post, when the sound of high, chattering voices caught her ear. She glanced up and saw two squirrels scampering down the trunk of the tree beside her.

"Four new babies!" the father squirrel said happily. "Isn't that wonderful?"

"Wonderful!" the mother squirrel agreed. "I can't wait to take them to all our favorite places in Wild Woods."

"Hello!" Rachel called to the squirrels. "We heard you talking about your new babies. We'd *love* to see them, wouldn't we, Kirsty?"

"Oh, yes!" Kirsty replied eagerly.

The squirrels glanced proudly at each other. "They're asleep in our nest in this tree," the father squirrel explained. "We'll show you the way."

Kirsty set her rake on the grass and Rachel put the lid on the can of paint, balancing her wet brush on top. Then they both grasped one of the lower branches of the tree and pulled themselves up. The squirrels led the way.

"Be careful, Kirsty," Rachel called as they climbed higher.

"Don't worry, I'm right behind you!" Kirsty assured her.

A little way up the tree, the squirrels stopped. The girls paused behind them and peeked into a hollow in the middle of the tree. There, nestled in a cozy bed of leaves, lay four baby squirrels. They were cuddled together, every one of them sound asleep.

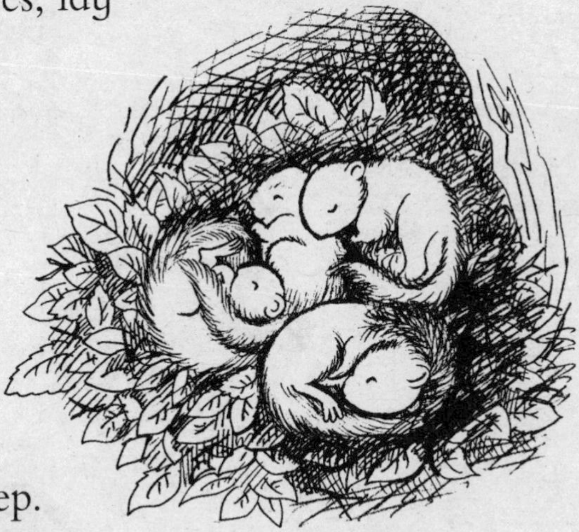

"They're adorable!" Kirsty whispered.

Smiling, Rachel nodded. It was then that she was surprised to see an unusual golden glow just above the nest. Her heart pounded excitedly as she looked more closely. Perched on a branch was a little fairy. She was dressed in a pink T-shirt printed with green leaves, a swishy gray skirt, and ankle boots.

"Oh, it's Kimberly the Koala Fairy!" Rachel whispered to Kirsty.

Their next fairy adventure was starting. Rachel couldn't wait to help Kimberly find her magic key chain.

Kimberly smiled at the girls, and then put her finger to her lips.

"We shouldn't wake these adorable squirrels," Kimberly said in a low voice. "But, girls, I'm desperate for your help. The goblins have kidnapped a baby koala named Kiki. They've taken her to Jack Frost's Ice Castle!"

The girls glanced at each other in dismay.

"We have to rescue her!" Rachel whispered.

"Let's go to the Ice Castle right away," Kirsty added.

"I knew I could rely on you, girls!" Kimberly said, relieved. "Fluffy the squirrel has offered to help. He's waiting for us at the Fairyland Nature Reserve, so that will be our first stop."

"Thank you for letting us see your beautiful babies," Kirsty told the squirrels as Kimberly lifted her wand.

"You're welcome," the mother squirrel replied. "Give our regards to Fluffy."

“We will!” said Rachel as they turned into fairies and Kimberly’s magic whirled them away to Fairyland.

Almost instantly they arrived at the Fairyland Nature Reserve to find Fluffy waiting for them.

“Hello, girls,” he called, scampering over to the three fairies. “Thank you very much for coming to help.”

"We need to hurry," Kimberly said anxiously. "I'm *so* worried about Kiki. Fluffy, will you lead the way?"

Fluffy nodded. The squirrel darted off, and Rachel, Kirsty, and Kimberly flew after him. They followed the squirrel through Fairyland, past the red-and-white toadstool houses and the winding river that sparkled in the sunlight.

But very soon they reached a much darker, colder place. Snow lay everywhere, and icicles hung from the withered, leafless trees. In the distance, the girls could see Jack Frost's Ice Castle high on a hill, the towers looming white against the gray sky.

"Almost there," Fluffy called. He tumbled down a snowy slope, with the girls and Kimberly flying nearby. He then raced through the frosted gates into the gardens of the Ice Castle.

The four friends hurried past the snow-covered pines and bushes, all cut into the shape of Jack Frost. Then Fluffy stopped beside a huge sign carved from a big block of ice. The sign said JACK FROST'S ZOO.

"Kiki might be in the koala enclosure," Kimberly said. "We should look right away."

But at that moment they heard the sound of an angry voice inside the zoo.

"What do you mean, you've let the koala escape? You silly goblins!"

"Jack Frost!" Kimberly whispered. "Hide!"

Fluffy, Kimberly, and the girls dashed behind the ice-block sign. They crouched down so they were out of sight. Kirsty peeked around the sign and saw Jack Frost stomp out of the zoo, his goblins scurrying behind him.

"That koala is the only animal you've managed to capture for my zoo, and now she's gone!" Jack Frost roared furiously. "Give me the magic key chain immediately"—Jack Frost held out his icy fingers—"and I'll go and find her myself."

The goblins glanced sheepishly at one another.

"The cute little koala liked the key chain so much, we let her play with it," one of the goblins mumbled. "And she took it with her!"

Jack Frost slapped his forehead in frustration. "Can't you do *anything* right?" he yelled.

"*He* gave it to her!" the shortest goblin said, pointing at another one.

"No, it was him!" the second goblin insisted, pointing at a third.

Jack Frost stamped away toward his Ice Castle. The goblins ran after him, still arguing.

"Let's check the koala enclosure," Kirsty suggested. "We may be able to find some clues to where Kiki went."

The girls and Kimberly followed Fluffy into the zoo. They flew past several empty animal enclosures until they found Kiki's. It was obvious right away that the baby koala wasn't there, but Rachel was surprised to see that the enclosure was decorated for a party.

There were bright green streamers and balloons everywhere, and a table set with party food. There was a large frosted cake, a big bowl of chips, a dish of ice cream, and other treats.

"It looks like the goblins were throwing a party for Kiki!" Rachel remarked.

"And look, there are paw prints in the

cake frosting," Kirsty pointed out. "Kiki *was* here!"

"I think the goblins have become really fond of cute little Kiki," Kimberly said with a smile. "They've given her things *they* like—a party, with lots of delicious food to eat. But koalas aren't goblins! What they really like to do is eat eucalyptus leaves and sleep in their mothers' pouches."

"I'm guessing that there aren't any eucalyptus trees around," Rachel said.

"No, there aren't," Kimberly confirmed. "So poor Kiki has nothing to eat. And worst of all, koalas are used to living in a much warmer part of the world. I'm really afraid that she'll freeze!"

"We can't let that happen!" Kirsty cried, horrified.

Just then they heard more angry shouting from the castle gardens.

"Jack Frost again!" Fluffy exclaimed.

"Let's go and see what happened," said Kimberly.

The four friends hurried out of the zoo in the direction of Jack Frost's voice. As they drew closer, they hid behind one of the snowy pines. Then they peered cautiously around the trunk.

Jack Frost was inspecting the bushes that had been shaped to look just like him. But Rachel could see that on one bush, a bite had been taken out of Jack Frost's enormous, leafy feet. On another bush, a chunk was missing from his long nose. Rachel nudged Kirsty and silently pointed this out to her friend.

"Who *dared* do this?" Jack Frost thundered while the goblins cowered against the bushes. "Someone is taking bites out of me, and I don't like it!" He shot the goblins a warning look. "I'm going to my room to take a royal nap," he snarled. "And you'd better find that koala before I wake up!"

Then Jack Frost stalked off.

"We have to find Kiki before the goblins do, so we can take her back home," Kirsty whispered. Meanwhile, the goblins were arguing about where to start their search.

Suddenly, a shower of snow floated down from above them. Thinking it had started snowing, Rachel glanced up at the sky.

But then she saw more snow fall from the top of one of the tall pines. At first, Rachel was puzzled. Was someone up there, knocking down the snow? The answer came to her in a flash.

"I think Kiki's up in that pine tree!" Rachel gasped as a few more flakes of snow drifted down. "I think she's tasting leaves, trying to find some eucalyptus—that's why she took bites out of the bushes!"

"Let's fly up there right away," Kirsty urged.

Kimberly and the girls zoomed up to the top of the pine tree while Fluffy ran up the trunk.

When they reached the top, Kirsty gave a cry of excitement.

"I see bite marks on these twigs!" she exclaimed. "But where's Kiki?"

"And I can see some pinecones that were nibbled on the next tree, too," Fluffy added. He ran along a branch and jumped into the other tree. Rachel, Kirsty, and Kimberly joined him, but there was no sign of the baby koala.

Kimberly and the girls began flitting between the pine trees, calling Kiki's name.

Meanwhile, Fluffy jumped from tree to tree, searching, too. The girls could see more bite marks and discarded leaves here and there, and so they followed Kiki's winding trail. It led them toward the tall pine tree that stood next to the top tower of the Ice Castle.

Then Kirsty's eyes widened as she spotted a shower of snowflakes falling from the tree. "There she is!" Kirsty exclaimed. She zoomed through the frosty air toward the tree. Rachel, Kimberly, and Fluffy followed her.

"Kiki?" Kirsty called softly. "Kiki, where are you?" But to Kirsty's intense disappointment, when she reached the tree, Kiki wasn't there.

"Where could Kiki have *gone*?" Kirsty sighed. "We've searched all the trees now."

"Maybe Kiki climbed down to the ground while we were looking for her up here," Rachel suggested.

"I'll go and see," Fluffy said, and he scampered off down the tree trunk.

At that moment, Rachel, Kirsty, and Kimberly heard a shout from an open window in the castle.

"HELP!"

"That's Jack Frost!" Kimberly declared, looking puzzled. "I wonder why he's yelling like that?"

"Let's check it out!" suggested Rachel.

Koala Chaos

Quickly, Kimberly, Rachel, and Kirsty flew through the open window and found themselves in Jack Frost's bedroom. To their surprise, the room was in a terrible state. Pajamas and slippers, as well as countless teddy bears, were tossed all over the floor. The comforter had been shredded to bits, and the pillowcases had been torn off the pillows. A giant poster of Jack Frost himself had also been ripped off the wall.

"What a mess!" Kirsty said.

"Where's Jack Frost?" Rachel wanted to know.

The bed was empty and Jack Frost was nowhere to be seen. A sound above their heads made the three friends glance up, and there, clinging to Jack Frost's icicle chandelier, they saw a sweet, furry little koala.

"Oh, we found Kiki!" Kimberly

gasped, relieved. "Poor thing, she must be freezing up there."

"Kirsty, isn't she just too cute?" Rachel exclaimed.

"She's lovely!" Kirsty agreed, staring at Kiki's big dark eyes, little black nose, and gorgeous fluffy ears. The girls were charmed by the baby koala and couldn't take their eyes off her.

Then Rachel noticed that Kiki was clutching something in her paw that shimmered with a magical golden glow.

"Kimberly, Kiki still has your key chain!" Rachel pointed out.

"So we found Kiki *and* my magic charm both safe and sound," Kimberly cried, smiling happily.

As they watched, Kiki began gently petting the key chain. The baby koala was obviously entranced by it, and Rachel realized that Kiki didn't seem to care about the cold at all.

"Kiki must have climbed in through the bedroom window while Jack Frost was asleep," Kimberly guessed. "And then she turned everything upside down, trying to find some eucalyptus leaves!"

"Kiki, are you all right?" Rachel asked as the three of them hovered in the air around the ice chandelier. "You must be cold and hungry."

But Kiki didn't answer. Her shining dark eyes were fixed on Kimberly's koala key chain as she tossed it playfully into the air and caught it again in her paws. Rachel could see that the baby koala was starting to shiver a little, though.

"We have to persuade Kiki to climb down from the chandelier before Jack Frost comes back," Kimberly told the girls anxiously. "Any ideas?"

Kirsty glanced around the room for inspiration. Then her eyes widened in surprise as she noticed an icy foot sticking out from underneath the bed.

“Jack Frost!” Kirsty exclaimed. She fluttered over to the bed and peered underneath. Jack Frost was crouched there, a look of fear on his face. “Why are you hiding?”

“No reason!” Jack Frost snapped, climbing out.

“You’re not afraid of this cute baby koala, are you?” Rachel asked.

"Of course not!" Jack Frost babbled, eyeing Kiki warily. But then he suddenly yelped with fright. "Keep that other creature away from me!" he roared.

Kirsty turned and saw Fluffy peeking in through the open window.

"That's only Fluffy, and he's a very friendly squirrel," Rachel explained. "He won't hurt you."

Jack Frost scowled at her. "I demand that you catch the koala and take her back to my zoo!" he yelled. "And when you've done that, you can clean up the dreadful mess she's made!"

"Come along, girls," Kimberly said, and the three of them flew back to the baby koala, who was still clinging to the chandelier. Jack Frost watched from a safe distance. "We'll try and persuade Kiki to come down, but we're not taking her back to the zoo, no matter what Jack Frost says!" Kimberly whispered.

"Hello, Kiki," Rachel said gently. "We've come to take you home."

Kiki glanced at them excitedly when she heard the word *home*. "Back to my mommy?" she asked hopefully in a sweet, grumbly little voice.

Before Rachel could answer, they heard the sound of running footsteps outside the bedroom. Then the door burst open with a crash! Rachel and Kirsty turned around quickly—what could be happening now?

Pillowcase Pouch

A crowd of eager goblins rushed in, tripping over their own feet as well as those of their friends. Kirsty could see they were all carrying bags of candy.

"We'll get the koala baby down!" shouted one of the goblins. He began jumping around under the chandelier, holding the treats out toward Kiki. The other goblins did the same.

"Come down, little koala," another goblin called, "and we'll give you some yummy candy!"

Kiki peered down at the goblins but didn't move.

"Candy! Candy!" the goblins chanted loudly, waving their bags in the air.

But the baby koala ignored them and began playing with Kimberly's key chain again. The goblins looked puzzled.

"Kiki doesn't eat candy," Kimberly explained to the goblins. "Koalas only like eucalyptus leaves."

"We don't have any of those," said one of the goblins.

"Never mind," said another. "We'll just have to eat all these treats ourselves!"

The goblins sat down in a corner and began greedily cramming the contents of the bags into their mouths.

"I want that koala out of here NOW and back in my zoo!" Jack Frost fumed, glaring at them. "Don't you have any other ideas?" But the goblins couldn't reply because their mouths were full of candy.

Kirsty glanced at Kiki, still swinging gently on the chandelier. To her alarm, she saw that the little koala's eyes were closing sleepily.

"Look, Kiki's really tired," Kirsty said urgently. "If she falls asleep, we'll *never* get her down from the chandelier."

Rachel frowned, wondering what they should do. Suddenly, Kimberly's words to the goblins popped into her head. *Koalas only like eucalyptus leaves . . .*

"Maybe we can tempt Kiki down with some eucalyptus leaves!" Rachel exclaimed. "Kimberly, could you create some with your magic?"

"That's a fantastic idea, Rachel!" Kimberly declared. With one swift flick of her wand, she conjured up a mist of fairy sparkles and instantly a pile of slender, scented green leaves appeared on the floor underneath the chandelier.

"Look, Kiki," Rachel called, pointing down at the floor. "Yummy eucalyptus leaves!"

Kiki opened her eyes, looking very excited. "Hooray!" she squeaked.

She jumped from the chandelier onto a nearby wardrobe and then climbed down the wardrobe to the floor, still clutching the magic charm. Jack Frost shrieked in fright.

"Grab that koala!" he ordered as he scooted underneath the bed again. But the goblins were enjoying their treats too much to notice.

Kiki sat down and eagerly began to munch the big pile of eucalyptus leaves.

"Those leaves look horrible!" one of the goblins remarked to another as he chomped on a chocolate. "I'm glad we've got candy instead."

"Poor Kiki's very hungry," Rachel said to Kimberly and Kirsty. "She's cold and sleepy, too. She must be missing her mom's warm, cozy pouch."

Kirsty nodded. "If we could make Kiki a little more comfortable, she might give up Kimberly's key chain," she said thoughtfully. "I was thinking, maybe we could find her some kind of pouch to snuggle into."

"Like what?" asked Rachel.

Kirsty looked around the bedroom and her eyes lit up as she spotted a pillowcase on the floor. "That would make a perfect pouch!" she said, pointing at it.

"And to make it extra warm, we could put some pieces of Jack Frost's comforter inside," Rachel suggested, glancing down at the shreds of soft fabric lying around them.

"Leave my comforter alone!" Jack Frost hollered from under the bed. But Kimberly and the girls ignored him. Between them, they collected scraps of the bedding and stuffed them inside the pillowcase.

"Kiki," Rachel called. "We made you a cozy pouch to sleep in!"

Kiki ate the last eucalyptus leaf, then, with a squeak of pleasure, she scampered across the room. Kimberly and the girls held the pillowcase open, and Kiki snuggled happily down inside it, cuddling the koala key chain close.

"Kiki needs something else to snuggle with, so we can have the key chain back," Kirsty murmured.

"What about one of Jack Frost's teddies?" Rachel suggested, glancing at the teddy bears strewn around the room. "He has lots of them."

Kirsty, Rachel, and Kimberly flew over to the bed and looked underneath. Jack Frost scowled at them.

"Can we give Kiki one of your teddies, please?" Kirsty asked politely.

"No way!" Jack Frost muttered.

"We'll help you clean up your room in return," Kimberly promised.

"Well, all right, then . . ." Jack Frost agreed reluctantly, and he handed them a tattered blue teddy bear that was lying under the bed next to him.

Between them, Kimberly and the girls carried the teddy over to Kiki. The baby koala was almost asleep.

"Kiki, here's a teddy for you to cuddle," Kirsty whispered.

Sleepily, Kiki let go of the key chain and held out her paws for the teddy. Kimberly flew joyfully down toward her charm, and the instant she touched it, it returned to its Fairyland size. Then she waved her wand and, in a flash, Jack Frost's room was neat and tidy again with everything in its place. Meanwhile, Rachel and Kirsty tucked Kiki and the teddy into the pouch together.

"Aww!" The goblins sighed as Kiki fell fast asleep. "She's so sweet!"

With a snort of disgust, Jack Frost crawled out from under the bed. "Goblins!" he shouted. "I order you to stop those fairies!"

Kiki Goes Home

Suddenly, Fluffy the squirrel leaped through the open window and landed on Jack Frost's bed. With a roar of fright, Jack Frost took to his heels and bolted from the room.

"Fluffy, thank you for your help," Kimberly said gratefully. "And you, too, girls. You've all been wonderful! But now we must take this sleepy little one home to her mom."

"I'll see you back in Fairyland, Kimberly," said Fluffy. "Good-bye, Rachel and Kirsty, and thanks for coming to our aid once again."

"Bye, Fluffy," Rachel said.

"Oh, and the squirrels in the Wild Woods and their babies send their regards!" Kirsty told him.

"I will go visit them very soon," Fluffy said with a smile. Then he jumped out of the open window and set off for Fairyland.

"Good-bye, little koala," the goblins called, crowding around the pouch as Kimberly waved her wand once more.

A soft mist of golden sparkles swirled around Kimberly, Kiki, and the girls, taking them swiftly to the koala's homeland. When the magic fairy dust cleared, Rachel and Kirsty saw that they were high in a eucalyptus tree. The tree was part of a huge forest overlooking the deep blue sea, and the sun was warm overhead.

Another koala was clinging to a branch of the tree near Kimberly and the girls, and her face lit up when she saw them.

"You brought my baby home!" the mother koala exclaimed happily. She hurried to Kiki and lifted her tenderly out of the pillowcase. Still holding Jack Frost's teddy, Kiki didn't wake up as her mother tucked her safely in her own pouch.

"Thank you," the mother koala said gratefully. "Would you like a snack of eucalyptus leaves before you go?"

"No, thank you," Rachel said with a smile. "We need to be getting home now that Kiki's back where she belongs."

"Let's go, girls," said Kimberly, raising her wand. The three of them waved good-bye to the mother koala, as Kimberly's fairy magic whisked them to Wild Woods once again.

When they arrived, the girls were back to their human-size. Kirsty picked up her rake and Rachel opened her paint pot.

"You helped me, so now it's my turn to help you!" Kimberly told them. A few magic sparkles produced another paintbrush so that Kirsty could help Rachel paint the last yellow arrows on the posts at the end of the trail. While they did this, Kimberly used her magic to clear the rest of the path.

As they were working, the squirrels bounded past them. "Hello," called the mother squirrel. "Our babies are awake now."

"Fluffy said he's coming to visit you," Kirsty told them, and both the squirrels looked very pleased.

Then, as the girls were finishing the last two arrows, they heard the sound of voices approaching on the trail.

"It's time I left!" Kimberly said with a smile. "You've been marvelous today, girls. Thank you again!" And she disappeared off to Fairyland.

Then Becky appeared with a group of visitors. She smiled widely when she saw the clear path and the freshly painted posts.

"Girls, you've done a fantastic job!" Becky announced. "The trail is all clear now, and so easy to follow."

The visitors murmured in agreement.

"Not like the trail Kiki left at the Ice Castle!" Rachel whispered to Kirsty as Becky opened her bag. Kirsty grinned at her friend.

"Nice work, girls!" Becky said, handing them each a new badge. The two badges had pictures of yellow arrows on them.

"I'll see you back at the wildlife center." Then she escorted the visitors away.

"What will happen at Wild Woods tomorrow?" Kirsty asked as they pinned the badges to their backpacks.

"Will there be another Baby Animal Rescue Fairy who needs our help?" Rachel wondered. "I really hope so—we only have two more magic key chains left to find!"

THE BABY ANIMAL RESCUE FAIRIES

Rachel and Kirsty found Mae, Kitty, Mara, Savannah, and Kimberly's missing magic key chains. Now it's time for them to help

Rosie the Honey Bear Fairy!

Join their next adventure in this special sneak peek . . .

Bees and Butterflies

"I wish it could be summer all year long," cheered Kirsty Tate.

She straightened up from filling her wheelbarrow and smiled at her best friend, Rachel Walker. Rachel dropped a small shovel into her own wheelbarrow and smiled back at Kirsty.

"Me too," she said, her cheeks pink from all her hard work. "And I wish we could help out at the nature reserve for longer, too. I love the animals so much!"

The girls were spending a week of their summer vacation helping at Wild Woods Nature Reserve as part of a team of junior rangers. Every day, they earned badges for their backpacks by doing special tasks. Becky, the head of the nature reserve, planned the tasks. That morning, she had thought of something especially fun for them to do together.

"I'd like you to plant shrubs along the bank of the stream," she had said. "The shrubs will attract bees and butterflies to the nature reserve. We depend on them to help keep the plants alive."

The girls had filled their wheelbarrows with pots of flowering shrubs, spades, short shovels, forks, and watering cans.

"We're ready, Becky!" called Kirsty.

"All right," Becky replied with a grin. "Follow me!"

She led them through the woods, and the wheelbarrows bumped over the branches and pinecones on the ground.

When they came out of the woods, the stream was straight ahead. Next to the clear, sparkling water they saw a row of little wooden houses on platforms.

"They look like fairy houses," said Kirsty excitedly.

She had spoken quietly, but Becky heard her and laughed.

"Yes," she said. "If fairies existed, I bet they'd love to live in one of these cute houses! Actually, they're beehives. The bees will use the nectar from the flowers you're planting to make honey."

Rachel and Kirsty smiled at each other. They had a secret that bonded them as best friends forever. They knew that fairies really did exist, and they had often visited Fairyland and shared adventures with their fairy friends.

Which Magical Fairies Have You Met?

SCHOLASTIC

Find all of your favorite fairy friends at
scholastic.com/rainbowmagic

RMSPECIAL14